BY DEBBIE PAKZABAN

ILLUSTRATED BY BONNIE LEMAIRE

Illustrated by Bonnie Lemaire

ISBN: 1493713736
ISBN 13: 9781493713738
Library of Congress Control Number: 2013920876
CreateSpace Independent Publishing Platform
North Charleston, South Carolina

There once was a boy named Pierre, but everyone called him *Lord Fancy Pants*. He lived with his mother and father in a magnificent palace on a hillside overlooking a beautiful village and green meadows.

Ever since he was a baby, his mother had embroidered LFP on the bottom of his diapers.

As he grew up, she continued to embroider on the bottom of all his pants so they would not get confused with his brothers' or sisters' pants on laundry day.

Lord Fancy Pants liked this very much and started insisting that his mother embroider giant letters in gold thread on the bottom of all of his fancy pants.

LFP, as was his nickname, decided that everyone should call him Lord Fancy Pants at all times. Or if they were in a hurry, LFP would do.

His mother began making him velvet pants with ruffles around the knees that were trimmed with exquisite lace from far-away lands.

LJP took this pant making process very seriously and had his mother hire the best seamstress in the kingdom to make beautiful clothes only for him. He would stand over the shoulder of the seamstress all day long and instruct her on what he wanted.

The gold thread that was used to make the large scrolling letters on his pants was the finest they could find. To show off the embroidery on his pants, he insisted that his jackets be short from behind.

Every afternoon he would go into town to show off his fancy pants. He would walk around the bazaar looking for more beautiful silks and velvets to make more fancy pants. His pants became famous and soon all the boys in the village were begging their mothers to make them fancy pants also!

One day while strolling through the bazaar,
a little boy threw a ball at LFP's feet.

Surprised, LFP eyed the boy up and down and was very displeased with the boy's plain brown ordinary pants. LFP turned his nose up, and walked away without uttering a word to the boy who only wanted to make friends. LFP had been very rude.

He was LORD FANCY PANTS, and he did not play with boys who were not in fancy pants!

He went home and told the seamstress she must make the fanciest pants the world has ever seen. In fact, he instructed her to make fancy pants for his little puppy as well. Now, that had never been thought of in his kingdom. He and his puppy Lancelot would be the fanciest of all!

The seamstress went to work on the fanciest pants in the world for a boy and his puppy. It took her thirty days to finish the pants. When Lord Fancy Pants finally saw them, he froze with happiness and began to cry with joy!

L.F.P.

They were made of gold fabric that was practically real gold, trimmed with diamonds everywhere. The ruffles had rubies sewn onto the lace, and the LFP on the back of the pants was embroidered with diamonds and pearls. They were, of course, the fanciest pants in the world!

He insisted she help him put them on immediately so he could show his family. As he put them on, he realized that all the gold and diamonds made the pants very heavy. They were also itchy and very stiff, so he could not walk very well in them. Not to worry, he thought, "I just need to break them in."

When it came time to put the pants on Lancelot, the puppy started to whimper. He was afraid to wear his fancy pants, so LFP held Lancelot down while the seamstress put the pants on the puppy. Lancelot could hardly move.

He went downstairs to show his father who was drinking tea at breakfast. His father almost choked on his tea and accidentally spat it out all over the table.

He could not stop laughing! His mother came running in to see what all the commotion was about? She dropped her tray of pancakes all over the floor and practically fell on the floor in laughter. His brothers and sisters ran in, saw him and also burst out in laughter.

His pants were stiff and went all the way up to his underarms. They were ballooned at the knees in big billowy gold poofs. They were so glittered with jewels that it sort of hurt your eyes to look at them too long.

But most importantly, LJP really could not walk very well. Nor could he sit down. He became very sad and ran to his mother for comfort. In between her fits of laughter she finally held him in her arms and said "Let's go change your pants into something more comfortable."

Off they went to change his pants. His mother found a pair of brown soft cotton pants that was in the bottom of his drawer. At first he frowned at the idea of non-fancy pants. After he put them on he could not believe how free he felt! He ran around his room jumping and feeling free of all things fancy.

He was feeling so relieved and happy that he decided to take Lancelot outside by the river and play some ball with his dog.

He left the pants on Lancelot, because he seemed to be getting use to the idea and could move around a lot easier. Besides, he just looked so handsome and regal in those doggy pants.

LJP started throwing the little toy ball to his doggy. As he threw it, the ball went into the water and Lancelot went in after it. As soon as the puppy jumped into the water, he began to sink and struggle. LJP jumped in to save him. LJP was not a good swimmer, so it turned out they were both in big trouble!

A boy who was fishing along the river bank heard the commotion, he ran to see what was happening. Without hesitation he jumped in and saved LJP and his puppy and dragged them to shore. LJP ripped off the silly dog pants and threw them in the river!!

As LJP and the puppy were catching their breath and shivering, LJP noticed the boy had been the boy in the village who had wanted to play with him. LJP felt ashamed and embarrassed. He apologized and thanked the boy over and over and the puppy licked his face with joy.

He asked the boy, whose name was Louie, if he could come to lunch and play at his house sometime. The boy agreed and was happy that he had saved LJP and his puppy.

LJP ran home to tell his parents what had happened. His mother and father suggested that he go into the village and give away all of his old silly fancy pants to people who never knew the joy of wearing such things. So they loaded up a very large wagon full of the fanciest pants in all the land.

Fancy Pants

When they got to the village, all the children gathered around waiting to get their own pair of fancy pants. So he gave away 500 pairs of fancy pants. Every little boy and girl in town had a few pair of fancy pants of their very own. He made the whole village so happy with his generosity.

He had one pair left: the new pair from that morning -- the fanciest pants in the world. No one wanted those? His mother and father insisted he keep them as a memory of his Fancy Pants Days.

Fancy Pants
FANCY P

Now that the business of fancy pants was behind him, Pierre went to play with Lancelot and Louie. As they all walked away, Louie had a twinkle in his eye and a skip in his step. Louie's mother had sewn his initials on the back his pants.

AUTHOR BIOGRAPHY
DEBBIE PAKZABAN

Debbie is an expert baker and story-teller who was raised by bears in an enchanted mountain forest in Utah. One day, while dancing with fairies, she ran into her future husband who had crashed his magic carpet into a tree while texting. They married and settled in Houston. Their two beautiful daughters, Lexy and Ashley, are the inspiration for Debbie's stories.

Made in the USA
Charleston, SC
11 July 2014